E
BAK

Baker, Sanna
Anderson.

Grandpa is a flyer.

301713

DATE			

DISCARD

BAKER & TAYLOR

Grandpa Is a Flyer

by Sanna Anderson Baker
paintings by Bill Farnsworth

Albert Whitman & Company
Morton Grove, Illinois

Cherry Hill
Kindergarten
Center

For Anne and her grandpa.
SAB

To my wife, Deborah, and my girls, Allison and Caitlin.
You have given me endless inspiration.
BF

Design by Sandy Newell.
Text is set in Weidemann Medium.

Text copyright © 1995 by Sanna Anderson Baker.
Illustrations copyright © 1995 by Bill Farnsworth.
Published in 1995 by Albert Whitman & Company,
6340 Oakton Street, Morton Grove, Illinois 60053.
Published simultaneously in Canada by
General Publishing, Limited, Toronto.
Printed in the United States of America.
10 9 8 7 6 5 4 3 2 1

Library of Congress Cataloging-in-Publication Data

Baker, Sanna Anderson.
Grandpa is a flyer / written by Sanna Anderson Baker ; illustrated by Bill Farnsworth.
p.   cm.
Summary: Anne's grandfather tells how he became interested in flying
in the early days of flight when barnstorming was popular.
ISBN 0-8075-3033-6
[1. Flight—Fiction. 2. Grandfathers—Fiction.] I. Farnsworth, Bill, ill. II. Title.
PZ7.B1755Gr 1995
[E]—dc20
301713
94-22008
CIP
AC

My father grew up on a small Midwest farm during the twenties and thirties. His hero was Charles Lindbergh who, in 1927, was the first to fly non-stop across the Atlantic Ocean alone.

Since flying with Lindbergh was out of the question, my father was determined to fly with a barnstormer. Barnstormers were pilots who landed in farmers' fields and sold rides to the local folk. Once he'd flown with a barnstormer, my father began to dream of being a flyer himself.

This is his story.

SAB

*W*hen we go to visit, Grandma always feeds us, no matter what time of day it is: rhubarb upside-down cakes, tuna broiler sandwiches, Swedish breakfast bundt cakes, fudge sundae bars.

My mother likes to stay at the table drinking coffee with Grandma, but it isn't long before Grandpa says to me, "Anne, do you want to take a hop?"

Grandpa is a flyer.

We drive to the airport at the edge of town where he keeps his plane. Inside the dark hangar it is echoey and cool. The huge door groans as we raise it. We push the plane into the sun, careful to keep it straight so the wing tips don't scrape the sides of the hangar.

I ask Grandpa, "How did you know you wanted to be a flyer?"
"That's a long story," he says.

I was out in the garden picking potato bugs. A plane—the first plane I'd ever seen—flew over. I was nine, and I thought the pilot was probably Charles Lindbergh. He was the first to fly across the Atlantic Ocean alone, and he was my hero. Named my dog Lindy after him, in fact.

Once I'd seen a plane in the sky I couldn't think about anything else. Every day my brother, Erik, and I rushed through our chores. We had to milk our cow, gather eggs, haul water, and bring in wood so we could get inside to hear "The Air Adventures of Jimmy Allen."

One day the noise of a plane nearly raised our roof. I banged out the screen door and squinted to see. It was so low and so loud, I knew the plane had to be landing. I begged Dad to take me.

Finally, when I promised to weed the garden, he said, "Get in!" We rattled up one dusty road and down another in the Model A until we saw the plane sitting in Conrad Johnson's field.

The pilot was dressed like Lindbergh in a flying suit and boots, but he had his goggles off, so I could see it wasn't Lindy. He was a barnstormer, a pilot who'd land in a farmer's field and sell rides.

"Ready for a ride, young man?" he asked me. I just shook my head. I didn't have any money, and I knew my dad didn't, either. But it didn't cost anything to look, and I looked over every inch of that Jenny.

After awhile our neighbor R.V. Carlson handed over his money and climbed into the cockpit. Seeing that plane take off was like watching a miracle.

That night I told Erik, "By next summer I'm going to fly."

The county board would give five cents a head for gophers because they were such pests, tunneling in the fields and feeding on roots. So Erik and I started a trap line. We carried the dead gophers home in a gunnysack, sprinkled them with salt to keep them, and saved them up until we had enough to make the five-mile hike to board member Bergsven's house.

When the gophers hibernated, we had to think of another way to make money. Saturdays that winter we split wood in the churchyard. Because Erik was five years older, he was the one allowed to sleep under the buffalo robe in the church furnace room, keeping the fire going all Saturday night so the church would be warm in the morning when the people came.

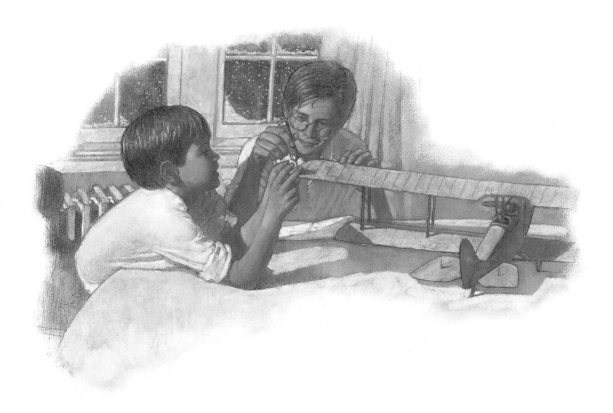

For Christmas that year our parents gave us a model plane—a Jenny with a five-foot wing span. Erik and I spent winter evenings working on it. I don't know if it was the feel of the smooth wood or just the way of boys with dreams, but we were in another world when we were working on that model. When it was done we hung it from our ceiling.

By the time summer came again we'd made enough money to fly. No matter where we were, we were always on the alert for the sound of a plane.

Finally one day, a plane circled overhead doing loops and rolls. It was a barnstormer for sure! We watched him set down in Gus Peterson's pasture, and then we ran to get our money.

Gus Peterson took his free ride for letting the pilot use his field. Then Paul Anderson and Verner Stanley had turns. Finally Erik forked over his money.

And then *I* was climbing into the cockpit! I couldn't hear a thing over the roar of the engine as we bumped down the field. My whole body vibrated, and I couldn't keep my teeth from clattering.

Suddenly we were in the air, as if we'd been cut loose.
Everything I knew—our house, the church, the farms around—looked
like miniatures while the rest of the world stretched on forever.

Seeing that made me want more than a ride. From that moment I knew that I wanted to be a flyer.

And then it was over. We hit the ground doing forty-five. Jennies didn't have brakes, so it took the length of Peterson's pasture to stop.

The crowd had dwindled. The pilot hopped out and said, "If I could get a ride into town with one of you folks, I'd be mighty obliged." Roy Wrolstad said he wouldn't mind.

Then the pilot turned to Erik and me. "Any chance I could hire you fellows for guards? I can't leave this Jenny alone with cows around. They love the dope that holds the cloth on her frame. Her sides'd be sagging by morning if Gus's cows were left to lick her all night."

He told us we could sleep on the wings. "Just keep the critters away. And if you clean 'er up–wash the cow dung off 'er belly where the prop blast sprayed it–I'll give you a ride in the morning and throw in a loop or two to boot," he promised.

You can bet we said yes. But then, there was telling Dad. If I went back home he might say I was too young, so I stayed with the plane while Erik went to talk with Dad.

I don't know just what Erik said, but he came back with a bag of sandwiches, a jar of milk, and some cookies, so I knew Dad couldn't be too mad.

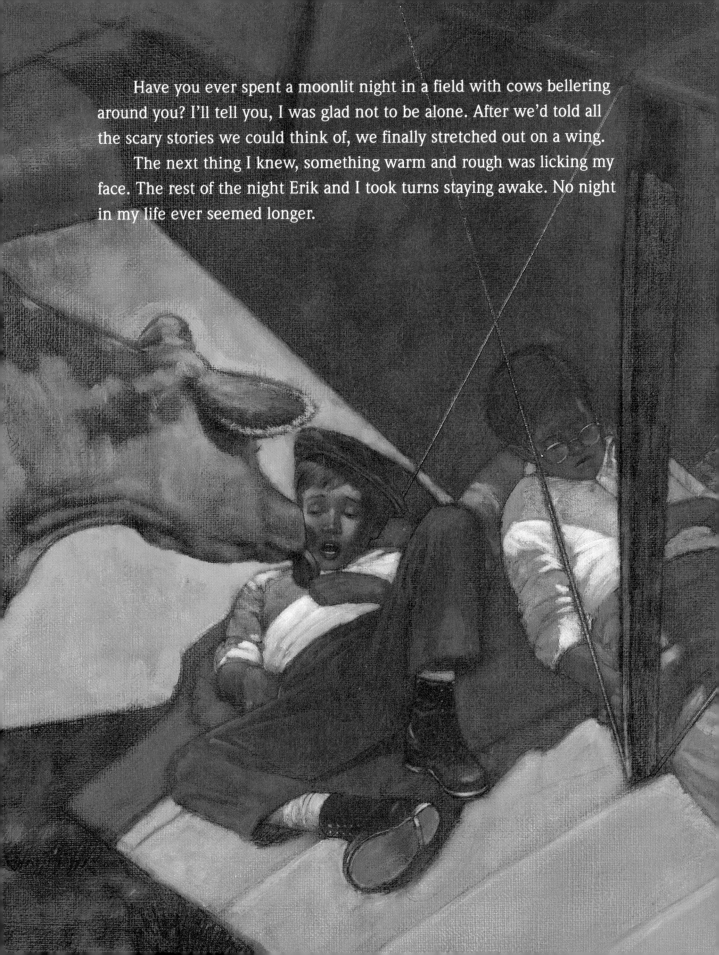

Have you ever spent a moonlit night in a field with cows bellering around you? I'll tell you, I was glad not to be alone. After we'd told all the scary stories we could think of, we finally stretched out on a wing.

The next thing I knew, something warm and rough was licking my face. The rest of the night Erik and I took turns staying awake. No night in my life ever seemed longer.

By the time the pilot came back in the morning, we had his old Jenny washed down and ready to go. He stowed a few groceries and handed Erik and me bottles of strawberry pop. First time we'd ever had pop.

If I thought my first ride was something, I really got a taste of flying this time: rolls, loops, stalls. Enough to make me wish I hadn't drunk pop. And enough to make me know I'd learn to fly someday.

I finished school, and then World War II came along. I was sent out to sea, but I never stopped thinking of flying.

When the war was over, I came home and married your grandma. We bought the farm, and when we could afford it, you can guess what I did!

I always thought your mother would learn to fly. She liked to come along with me—used to help me get the plane out of the hangar just like you do. But she didn't turn out to be a flyer.

"Now what say we stop talking *about it and* do *some flying?"*
Grandpa asks with a wink. We climb into the plane and buckle up.

"All clear!" Grandpa shouts. The propeller whirs, then whirls so
fast you can't see the blades.

We roar down the runway, headed straight for the trees. Just in
time, we lift off.

In seconds the land below looks like a quilt, squares of colored fields stitched together with gravel roads. Rivers turn to ribbons, clouds tower like mountains.

"Maybe someday you'll get yourself some wings!" Grandpa shouts over the engine's roar.

Someday maybe I will.